No David

David was a little boy who always found himself in trouble. His messy hair and big smile were a clear sign that mischief was never far behind.

David, no!" his mother would shout, as she saw him running through the house with muddy shoes, leaving dirty footprints everywhere.

One day, David decided to draw on the walls. With a crayon in his hand, he covered the white walls with squiggles and shapes. "No, David!" his mother cried out when she saw the mess.

At dinner, David couldn't sit still. He played with his food, making faces and noises. "No, David!" his mother warned, as peas flew off his plate and onto the floor.

Bath time was another adventure. David splashed water everywhere, soaking the bathroom floor. "No, David!" echoed through the house as the water dripped into the hallway.

When it was bedtime, David didn't want to sleep. He jumped on his bed, making it squeak loudly. "No, David!" his mother said, trying to tuck him in.

One day, David's curiosity led him to the kitchen. He tried to reach the cookie jar on the top shelf. "No, David!" his mother yelled, catching him just in time before he could knock it over.

David loved playing outside, but he often forgot to listen. He ran into the street to chase a ball. "No, David!" his mother called out, running after him.

Despite all the "No, David!" moments, there was something special about David's heart. He always smiled, even when he knew he was in trouble.

One evening,
after a long day
of "No, David!"
his mother sat
down next to him.
She looked into
his big, innocent
eyes and said,
"David, yes."

David was surprised. "Yes, David, you are loved," she whispered as she hugged him tight.

And even though David continued to find himself in all sorts of trouble, he always knew that, no matter what, his mother loved him very much.

Made in the USA
Columbia, SC
29 November 2024

47923546R00015